A Note to Parents & Caregivers—

Reading Stars books are designed to build confidence in the earliest of readers. Relying on word repetition and visual cues, each book features fewer than 50 words.

You can help your child develop a lifetime love of reading right from the very start. Here are some ways to help your beginning reader get going:

⭐ Read the book aloud as a first introduction

 Run your fingers below the words as you read each line

 Give your child the chance to finish the sentences or read repeating words while you read the rest.

⭐ Encourage your child to read aloud every day!

Every Child can be a Reading Star!

Published in the United States by Xist Publishing
www.xistpublishing.com

First Edition
eISBN: 978-1-5324-3197-5
Paperback ISBN: 978-1-5324-3198-2
Hardcover ISBN: 978-1-5324-3199-9
Printed in the United States of America

Hog Dog

Audrey Bea

Franko Sviatoslav

xist Publishing

Look! A dog.

It is hard to see
through the fog.

It may be a hog.

It looks like it is a hog.

It has a head like a hog.

It has legs like a hog.

It even has a tail
like a hog.

But it must be a dog!

It has a tongue
like a dog.

It has ears like a dog

It is hard to see in all the fog.

I think it is a hog dog.

I am a Reading Star
because I can read the
words in this book:

a	it
all	legs
be	like
but	look
dog	looks
ears	may
even	must
fog	see
hard	tail
has	the
head	think
hog	through
I	to
in	tongue
is	

CPSIA information can be obtained
at www.ICGtesting.com
Printed in the USA
LVHW072017071221
705525LV00005B/138